AF254830

BEYOND BOUNDARIES

by
Trevor P. Kwain

Published by Threepeppers Publishing
Translated by Carol Winteringham

2nd Edition – February 2017
First published in Italian in Great Britain in 2012

ISBN: 978-0-9957274-2-7

www.3peppers.co.uk

www.trevorpkwain.org

INDEX

The old watchman

The town of Urbina was already immersed in darkness. No light came from the windows, everything was switched off, all the population was fast asleep. Silence reigned in the streets, only once in a while the eyes of a cat or dog sparkled in the narrow alleyways sparsely lit by the moon, but no sounds were made. Night had fallen engulfing everything with its black cloak, bringing with it who knows what night creature; those creatures that exist in the myths and legends the world over.

However, in that darkness there was a yellowish light outlining the edges of the town. Indeed, not far from it stood the Urza power station, up on a hill. It was a plain building the colour of red fire. Its foundations were pillars which absorbed a certain amount of thermal energy from the ground. It was a modest amount but sufficient for Urbina and some of its surrounding farms. It was active twenty hours a day so at night it was the only source of light in that area and it looked like a rare aurora borealis. The inhabitants of Urbina were in no way irritated by this light, rather they jealously took care of their power station as it was their one and only source of survival and besides it was like having an ace up their sleeve considering the importance of the industrial-war sector. It had increased in importance especially since the Technical Revolution had invaded the continent. For this reason, there was always a watchman there who stood by the gates watching over the station, day and night. The man was wearing a tunic and he had now become to look extremely shabby. When the power station was first opened, the town council immediately looked for a suitable watchman; he was the only one who came forward as most people discarded the idea as being a tiring job. He was a stranger to the town folk, no one had ever seen his face, as it was always covered by a dusty hood. Most people thought he must have been an old man. Indeed, his hands were large and rough, he could barely walk and he was always out of breath. The town council was in no way concerned about this and he was taken on; since that day he has always been there, observing the power station and the town as if he was a statue. Because of his appearance, the locals had given him the nickname of the Rag Man.

That night the Rag Man was standing still gazing up at the winter sky. The only sounds to be heard came from the crickets and the low hum coming from the basement of the power station. Suddenly the Rag Man noticed something on the road leading up to the station almost half a mile from him; it was an enormous figure, the most frightening ever seen in those lands. It approached slowly, plodding his way with heavy footsteps, making acute grunting sounds every now and then. His footsteps made the ground tremble as the distance between the Rag Man and the silhouette diminished. Then the light coming from the power station allowed the Rag Man to make out the being which was now only a few steps away. It was a powerful creature, he reckoned, as it approached. It must have been twice the height of the Rag Man, it crawled on four legs and had a saggy grey coloured skin. A long trunk like nose hung down extending from his small tired eyes and on either side were two long curved tusks. The Rag Man was surprised but his expression was hidden by his hood. Then a voice spoke.

'Hey, old man, open the gate we need to do overtime!'

The old watchman moved to the side to see better and noticed that sitting on the creature's back were two women with long hair. One with dark hair and skin, as dark as night itself that turned to a bronze colour under the strong light of the station; the other was pale, both her hair and skin were a deathly white. They both wore a waistcoat and trousers and their necks were decorated with necklaces and chains of every kind.

'Hey, old man, aren't you with it? We have to go in!' repeated the pale girl in an annoyed tone.

The two girls slid off down the sides of the creature; they had slim young bodies. They headed for the gate of the power station but the Rag Man would not let them pass and he blocked their way.

'Hey, are you mad? They've just called us out it's urgent and we have to do a silly check. There's no need for me to tell you how annoying it is, and you're preventing us from entering?' shouted the pale girl.

She was about to push him aside when the Rag Man raised his arm, waved his finger and touched the girl's jewels. He then picked up a stick and started writing something in the dusty track. He wrote in large print.

CUOMBAJJ WITCHES

The old man lifted his head and brandished the stick in front of his chest as if he were about to start combat. The two girls were shocked, disorientated. Then after a long silence the dark-skinned girl spoke.

'You know us! You know who we are! For all the bat's wings who on earth are you?'

'It doesn't matter,' interrupted the other girl. 'whoever puts themselves between us and power ends up well and truly dead.'

The girl raised her eyes up to the sky and after saying a series of meaningless phrases, the wind grew and began to blow stronger and stronger, creating a large cloud of dust between the Rag Man and the young witch. The old watchman stepped back leaning on his stick. The cloud quickly started to condense and take on some kind of form although its outline was still very vague. Then the layer of sand solidified and out of it appeared a sea snake which twisted its way up in front of the old man. The long slimy body twisted and turned in a never-ending swirl but its head stayed still staring at the watchman in his eyes. Its green crest and purple eyes were terrifying. The snakes wide open mouth revealed all of its tiny sharp teeth. Bits of flesh were stuck between them: traces of his last meal. However, the Rag Man did not falter, he put the palm of his hand to his chin and blew. This strange, mysterious puff created another strong wind. The snake felt dizzy and fell like a house of cards; only a tiny mound of sand remained and that too quickly disappeared. The old man was alone again in front of the power station but he looked different from before. His tunic was no longer a mass of rags but more of an intense blue which shone brightly in the clear light of the power station. The Rag Man put his hands on his hood and slowly lifted it up. Beneath the hood was a young face with azure eyes and blond hair, a sort of magic air which surprised the two witches.

'So, that's why he managed to defeat us! He's a magician!' said the white witch in a hysterical voice.

'A wizard from the Blue Caverns. old maids!' he replied resolute. 'Elephants and sea snakes don't exist in these regions. I have been waiting a long time for the right moment to get back what was stolen from me and your silly games won't stop me. The energetic flare belonged to my people. The Technical Revolution has ruined everything, all the traditions of wizards that my ancestors had handed down from generation to generation.'

'Don't think it's all over!'

This time it was the black witch who spoke raising her arms up to the sky. In that precise moment, the earth began to tremble and both of the witches' faces turned to stare at the power station which began to sway under the effect of the tremble. The wizard jumped round. The huge structure was about to crumble; tentacles of earth rose out of the ground covering the foundations: the power station was losing all its strength and the energy would have disappeared into the air. The wizard simply couldn't allow his hard work and the work of his people of all the past years to dissipate into thin air. He shut his eyes and concentrated. He too raised his arms up toward the sky; all the chaos around him disappeared. His spread-out arms started to vibrate; they looked as if they were magnets that attracted all the energy of the power station and now a large ball of fire had formed over his head. Suddenly a flash of lightning struck a spot on the hillside and an intense glare illuminated the whole plain for several seconds. The witches, the elephant and the wizard himself fell to the ground and soon after everything turned dark and silent again.

It was almost dawn and no sound was to be heard, even the crickets were hardly perceivable. The power station was switched off, and without any source of energy, the surrounding area was desolate. There was the odd light in a few windows in Urbina as some of the population had been terrified by the explosion. The first to arrive on the scene were the night vigilantes armed with their forks and oil lamps. They only thing they came across was a strange grey creature running furiously off over the hill. The vigilantes saw a circle of burnt ground still smoking but nothing else. So, no one could give a satisfactory explanation. The watchman had disappeared and he was in fact soon forgotten because his presence was no longer of any importance. Today the station is used as a school for scientists and visited by a large number of people from all over the world who are keen to see this monument to the Technical Revolution. The inhabitants of Urbina have lost something important but at the same time they have found something new and just as profitable. Man will never stop when faced with obstacles. He will do his best every time to overcome them, whatever it may cost.

The town of Urbina is now back to its peaceful normality, just like it used to be. According to the elders of the town, they think they can see some kind of light coming from the power station which lights up the whole surrounding area, even though there are no light sources for miles around. Maybe they should look upward to the northern sky where a small white spot releases an intense light every winter. It is the light of the Wizards of the Blue Caverns and even today it still guides man in his feats.

The secret of Talibah

The temple of Talibah lies in the middle of a tropical jungle far from the civilized world and has been uninhabited for centuries. Nobody knows who built it; maybe it was built by a prehistoric population that disappeared without leaving any trace. The local people believe it to be an evil place still haunted by the ghosts of ancient tribes who are ready to slaughter whoever tries to approach it. Many people have set off in order to unveil its mystery never to return. And that was how the legend came to be.

Commander O'Donagh was also about to become a legend although he did not yet know it. Just like every other soldier, he did not have the time to sit around and fantasise about his future, his only objective was to fulfil the mission entrusted to him in the shortest time possible. The port of Maracao was extremely busy that morning: hundreds of slaves, merchants, soldiers were rushing backward and forward up and down the quay of the port. The commander and his platoon had just landed and the first thing that came to his mind was to get away as fast as he could from that hellish place. With some difficulty, they managed to reach parts of the village where life seemed a little calmer. Quite the opposite, the outskirts were totally deserted. There was the odd young boy running around the streets but no one else. Soon they were completely alone. The savannah had been replaced by large trees which then led to a jungle which got thicker and thicker as they proceeded. The sun had started to go down behind the horizon but for the group of foot soldiers it had been gone for quite a while leaving them with just a plain blue sky above them. However, when night came, the platoon was swallowed up by the darkness of the jungle. Two of the foot soldiers asked if they could make camp but the commander knew well that such a short and simple rest would be extremely dangerous for him and his men. He said nothing, he just carried on walking, guided by the light coming from his lamp; the only light they had in that silent jungle darkness. They walked and walked keeping pace in silence. Each and every one of them was lost in their own thoughts anxious to end this mission. All of a sudden, O'Donagh thought he heard a voice saying 'Stop!'. He turned to face the foot soldier at his side who did not seem to have heard anything. So, he stopped, raised his arm, and after observing the jungle he spoke to the foot soldiers.

'Stop! Let's camp here for the night!'

Next morning the sun was high in the sky. The jungle looked so different under the effect of daylight. The commander was already up and about, deep in thought. On one hand, he was glad the night had passed without any trouble, but on the other hand, he was surprised to see two empty blankets. Two footmen had deserted camp; only the two of them were left and would have to do whatever was necessary. As soon as the other was ready, they set off again on their journey. While they were trying to find a suitable opening in the thick vegetation, the commander's thoughts went back to the strange dream he had had that night. He had dreamed about a handsome, magnificent hawk that could see everything, high up above the jungle, and a huge dragon down below, who was threatening to kill him. More than a dream, it was a nightmare, a bad dream that had made the commander wake up in a sweat.

It was early morning and the weak sun already shone in the sky, O'Donagh lifted his head to see and there he saw the hawk handsome and majestic hovering directly above them. The hawk seemed to be moving with them as if it was leading them in some way. At a certain point, the hawk flew down to the right and the commander shouted to his soldier.

'Go right!'

His decision was advantageous because after a few hundred metres they came across a wide plain. In front of them a massive impressive building rose up. It was the Temple of Talibah. It was as fascinating as it was frightening. It did not seem to have a door, just a large opening. Inside, it was not in total darkness, there was just enough light coming from the opening to be able to see the central hall before them. There was a row of torches with feeble flames on each side of the hall; they seemed immune to the strong wind that was blowing from a hole in the roof. In the middle of the hall there was a gigantic statue that stretched up to the ceiling and touched the sky. Its face was in the shade so it was difficult to make out its lineaments while its body was in the light and they could see strange figures and signs on it. Its powerful arms were set as if to balance itself and two smaller statues were hanging from its large hands by ropes: a warrior on the one hand and a dragon on the other. The giant statue was not the only presence in the temple, around it lay tons of pure gold that sparkled in the torchlight.

The footman rushed forward to admire that mountain of wealth but the commander on the other hand did not take much notice as he was taken in by the writing. They were simple hieroglyphics interrupted here and there with pictures of priests and worshippers. O'Donagh started to translate even if he did not feel particularly at ease with the evil dragon's eyes staring at him: that same dragon he had dreamt about the night before. This was what was written on the statue.

In the beginning the great god Talibah created Man. Seeing that Man lived harmoniously with Nature, Talibah gave him fire and gold. With one, Man would have given life to the Great Civilisation and the other would have guaranteed happiness and splendour. However, Man began to argue and this made Talibah angry. He was so angry he decided to divide Man's soul in two parts; a good one and a bad one which would have persecuted the good side forever more. Therefore, leave every vice, every object of perdition at Talibah's feet, or evil would have the upper hand....

All of a sudden, a flash of lightning filled the sky. The commander looked up. The sky had turned purple, a dark purple. He noticed the statue of the dragon was now slightly raised and the one of the warrior a bit lower. In a flash the footman struck him from behind with his sword which went straight through him coming out on the other side of his body. Bleeding O'Donagh just managed to turn before falling to the ground. Just enough time to see the footman's hands full of gold coins and eyes full of greediness. At that same precise moment, the dragon's eyes shone bright red. The words on the statue continued.

...but Man, is not capable of controlling himself and others. Talibah had warned him, but Man is and always will be the victim of his own fate. He will never be able to flee from the strings of destiny, not even if he has a pair of scissors.

A full treasure chest, an empty man

The boat drifted slowly down the river. The light brown-haired young man rowed in rhythmical strokes over the dark and restless waters. The sky was grey and dull, the trees lining the riverbank were bright green, but wilting. The only sound to be heard was the skimming of the oar over the water's surface, a short spurt and that was it. The young man was strong and adventurous for his age, his face determined, fearless, looking straight ahead. However, it was no empty glance, that boy was looking for something, you could see it in his eyes, that look of expectancy and wonder awaiting something he had been searching for, for a long time. A tree trunk stuck out of the water at this point, bent over a bit like a bridge across the river. It looked as if it was about to fall into the water but who knows how many years it had been like that in that same position, who knows how many people had seen it like that and thought the same thing. Misguided, as the power of Nature was boundless.

The tiny figure sitting on the trunk, a goblin, one of the many creatures of the wood, thought the same thing. At that moment his hands were juggling with a bundle of entrails, which made the young man come to a halt; he simply could not carry on faced with that strange sight. The young man approached until he was right under the trunk although the goblin did not seem to have noticed him.

'Where are you heading for?' asked the goblin suddenly.

'And who might you be?' asked the young man.

'I'm the one asking the questions around here. Where are you going?'

'My resting place is where many men look within Nature itself.'

'Don't try and be funny. I am the one who talks in riddles here. You are very young and already too ambitious. Maybe you want to know how your search for the Mana Treasure chest will end up?'

'How on earth did you know that, goblin?'

The goblin chuckled.

'Take a look at this bundle of entrails. It doesn't seem like much but it does hold a meaning.' said the goblin.

'I'm not interested in any anatomy lessons, thank you!' the young man answered rudely.

'Be careful! Too much pride and arrogance won't get you anywhere.' warned the goblin.

'You won't stop me, wrinkled old goblin. You won't block my way!' cried the young man angrily and he passed under the trunk leaving the goblin behind him.

'I'll say that again.' repeated the goblin a little worried this time. 'Don't be in such a hurry. Look carefully at the road you are taking, not the destination. Sometimes the two don't coincide.'

By this time the young man was far off and as the Rocky Mountains came closer, his ambition grew.

According to the Scriptures, the Treasure chest lay there among the red scarlet and purple stones protected by the Silver Knights. The young man tied up his boat in an inlet at the foot of the mountain range. He was not afraid of the magnificence of the rocky mass, which stretched up before him, into the amber sky. Without second thoughts, he started to climb and climb and climb. He must have climbed for hours and that twinkle in his eye became even stronger. His yearning for knowledge was full of greed and pride; it seemed almost abnormal but innate at the same time. After hours of walking, he came to the end of the path but the peak turned out to be useless for what he had been hoping to come across. A long stretch of snowy mountain peaks extended before him and just as many stretched out behind. The treasure chest could be anywhere, behind any grey rock, under any mantle of snow. He was willing to spend a lifetime just to find it. The young man fell to his knees out of desperation, out of anger. He had set off on this long walk, this climb, only to hear the words 'Carry on boy, just a bit more effort'. Yes, one more try, and one more and so on until he was at the end of his tether, drained of all his strength. All this effort for nothing.

Then all at once, a gust of wind blew its gelid call. The freezing cold came over him and he was left standing completely still with all his regrets. Out of nowhere, four men appeared, accompanied by the wind and surrounded him on all four sides. All four of them wore silver armour, once bright and shiny, now worn out and lacking lustre. They all lifted their swords together and unleashed them with swift decisive strokes that echoed all around rather like a ghost of the past coming to haunt us. The young man's regrets were so real they hit him in one stroke. It is like a poison, which creeps its way into our minds so quickly before you even realise it and then it is too late to do anything about it. His body lay there on the ground prey for the crows and jackals.

Even today, those adventurers who go searching for the Mana Treasure chest see his shadow lost amid the thousand others in the candid snow. All of them ambitious, empty people who lose what they have inside them, only to try and gain what is on the outside. One day if you have time, take a walk up to the top of that mountain and you will come across all the bodies, all without guts. It is said that the goblin loves to collect them but hardly any one takes it seriously.

The dragon who knew too much

Mythology and legends cover every possible phenomenon that Man does not know about or cannot explain. Monsters, dragons, winged creatures, magical and mysterious figures have haunted the pages of our books for centuries with their terrible faces and frightening shrieks. Examples to be avoided and even fight. But why?

One small dragon, Teferi, was a harmless orange coloured dragon in full youth. He had always lived with his peers in the land of Weatherlight, a tiny swampy area which fortunately still remained uncontaminated, far from man and all his devilry. Teferi was always on the move. He flew here and there over the stagnating waters searching and exploring every tiny thing in his small world. He was so full of energy he was capable of flying and hopping around for hours on end, tirelessly.

One morning, feeling at his usual full strength, he pushed himself to reach the edge of his territory where the dry land replaced the muddy waters of Weatherlight. Teferi noticed that on the edge of the forest there was a small brick tower. Curious to see it close up he glided gently down in front of it. It was nothing but a simple brick tower, maybe a shelter for animals or even men except there was a gold statue perched on its top which shone in the hot sun. Teferi could not make out its shape; it did not even seem to have one. It stood on four paws but its body-shape was incomprehensible, a tangle of unidentifiable golden parts. Teferi tried to make some sense of it but the more he looked, the more confused he became. Then, he noticed an array of writings running along the bricks, down the walls as if the tower was a kind of book. The dragon became even more curious and so he started to decipher the series of images and symbols that filled the tower walls. At first sight, there did not seem to be a beginning and an end and surely, the interpretation had to be made by the reader himself. Toward dusk Teferi had completed reading the whole tower and his brain had accumulated a large number of notions from philosophy to grammar, from history to science, from mathematics to history. By now, he could distinguish physics phenomena and come up with their respective laws. He managed to solve complicated mathematical calculations and build real metaphysical concepts. An illuminated mind, that is what he had become, he knew things nobody else knew. He was an intellectual, superior to the other dragons. Teferi, taken by surprise, flew up overcome by joy and headed for home darting through the wind and clouds just like the plane designed by a certain Leonardo. It was deep into the night when he got back home, the swampland was silent and all the dragons were fast asleep by now. Teferi was still excited about his discovery but decided to wait until morning before putting his new intelligence to the test.

Next morning Teferi took up being an orator and he spoke non -stop all day, explaining his theories to the other dragons and confirming them himself in front of the absent faces of his listeners. The small dragon felt as if he were the centre of attention, getting all the limelight, pleased to be able to convey his knowledge to the others but he also felt something was missing. He was the only one talking, there was no dialogue or debate with his audience (according to the thoughts of a certain figure named Plato), and it was as if he was the only one who existed. What sense was there talking about metaphysics, poetry, astronomy, eschatological processes, if those in front of him were silent and illiterate? So, he decided to take all his tribe up to the tower. The dragons spent all day absorbing the writings and by the time dusk came the whole dragon community was able to understand and reflect. Teferi, feeling satisfied by the leaps and bounds his people had made, he perched himself on the top of the tower and in a loud voice started his speech. Unfortunately, no one stayed to listen to him; they could not waste their time staying there, there was a whole lot of topics to deal with and explore. Very quickly, the tower emptied as the dragons all went about their business; some set about studying the plants of the forest, others discussed the development this knowledge would have brought them and so the first ideologies were born. Then the first discords were unleashed, the first arguments and at the end a real and proper battle exploded in a short time. The dragons split into factions to defend their ideas at all costs. The conflict lasted all night with fire and flames and Teferi was witness to it all. Saddened by the whole event and worried about how he had let the situation get out of hand, he turned his back on the battlefield and disappeared into the darkness.

The morning after a thick mist had come down and settled over the smelly waters of Weatherlight. Hundred s of dragons lay dead or hurt around the tower. Those thirsty for blood and power had left in search of new lands. Very few had remained on the battle scene. So it was that, from that day the dragons had chosen different directions, each and every one of them had lost the innocence of once upon a time. The light of reason had made them blind without a soul to confide in. Now they stay in the darkness of their dens, ready to devastate the countryside and villages, frightening women, children and challenging kings and knights. They stay there in the dark on a pile of broken bones and crushed skulls with their skin scratched and their eyes glaring with anger, shouting the fiery lament of those who always want to be in the right.

The cross of Saint Donizio

Dardania is a town in the shape of a cross, most certainly not unique in its style but having a certain originality: every year an exhibition of antiques takes place in the centre of the large cross. The town is grand, the ethnic races that have passed through Dardania have been many, millions in fact. There had never been a person to pass through here without concluding a good deal, a bargain or at least Sir Beagle thought so, as he walked through the West gateway of the town.

The streets were crowded. Many people had come to Dardania that morning and chaos already reigned: the shouting, the grinding of the caravans, the neighing of the horses and grating of steel, it certainly was not a quiet place to do business and make purchases. It was not really worth making all the effort to go there when you saw what kind of goods were on sale on the stalls: brass lamps, ceramic vases, charms, bracelets, parchments but there were some rather old looking objects which many considered as valuable as pure gold. Of course, Sir Beagle had not come to town for anything in particular but only to browse, to see whether there was anything interesting. He thought he had a flair for bargains, even though some of his friends had said they had seen him purchasing a blind mule in exchange for an Egyptian parchment.

The main street was busy with the comings and goings of the merchants and at that moment Sir Beagle was engaged in scrutinising a bronze hourglass. All at once, a man sprung out of nowhere in the crowd, running like mad and then he grasped hold of Sir Beagle who was shocked. Scared to death, he spun round and saw this poor man dressed in rags, sweating, with scars all over his face, tired eyes, carrying a small cross. Suddenly without waiting a second, he pronounced a few words, an almost imperceptible hiss.

'Would…would you…like to purchase…' said the man out of breath. '…this artefact…sir?'

Sir Beagle opened his eyes wide and looked at the cross again. What a beautiful object! A splendid cross, carved in wood, ebony to be precise. This really did look like a bargain. He was so fascinated by this object that he no longer heard the voices of the merchants. Then the man spoke again in a louder tone of voice and Sir Beagle came back to his senses, to real life.

'Well, after what I told you, are you interested in buying the Cross of St. Donizio?'

'What? Well...of course I will buy it. I'm not as foolish as you to give away such a precious object.'

The man was amazed. Half a smile appeared on his lips and his tired eyes suddenly lit up with joy. He gave a heart breaking cry which shocked everyone around who heard him. The man seemed to be going crazy, he leaped and embraced everyone around him then all of a sudden, he rushed to the other side from where he had come from and disappeared again into the crowd. Sir Beagle was bewildered; the man could still be heard singing at the bottom of the street even though he hadn't realized he had left the cross behind. He really had come across a bargain. Maybe he was wrong.

For the rest of the day Sir Beagle wandered around Dardania but his mind was continuously on the cross. When nightfall had started to descend on the streets, he decided to return home through the West gateway from where he had come. There was a quiet moment with not many people around so he took the opportunity to leave and avoid all the crowds who would soon be going home too. As soon as he took a step to pass through the gateway, a thick cloud appeared before him- Sir Beagle took a step back. From out of the cloud came the shape of a shark which startled Sir Beagle. He was still under shock when the shark started to speak.

'Man, do not leave the town, do not allow water to abandon this place, the equilibrium must never be broken…'

As quickly as the shark had appeared, it disappeared again and in its place a barrier of fire flared up high into the sky. Sir Beagle rubbed his eyes, but the fire was still there; it was no hallucination, he could even feel the heat of the flames on his skin. He stepped backward slowly and frightened by it all, he ran as quickly as possible toward the North gateway. This gateway was quiet, no one around, maybe it was dinner time by now. It was a quiet area, no noise, no wind. Sir Beagle hurried to cross through the gateway, still confused by what had happened before, but no sooner had he put his foot under the mighty arch another cloud appeared. This time two green goblins came out and they spoke.

'Man, do not leave this town, do not allow land to abandon this place, the equilibrium must never be broken…'

And they disappeared in a flash. Then came another barrier of fire, twice the height of the first, blocking the passage. Sir Beagle was even more terrified and could do nothing but flee, this time toward the East gateway. Still under shock he ran like mad, his heart beating, pulsating through the silent streets of Dardania.

At the East gateway, the situation was identical: absolute silence. The only sound, just about audible, was the squeaking of a sign, but apart from that, the town now seemed deserted. Sir Beagle was still in a panic but he had not lost all control. Indeed, before stepping through the gateway he thought carefully and looked around him, trying to make some kind of logical sense out of it.

Unfortunately, it came to nothing, as there was nothing strange, only an old wooden gateway. Not knowing what to do he walked through the gateway, and yet again a cloud appeared before him and blocked his way. Out of the clouds came another figure, a man wrapped in a tunic of exotic colours and decorated with thousands of necklaces and jewels. At the same time, a strong gust of wind started to blow but the voice of the figure managed to overpower the wind.

'Man, do not leave the town, do not allow air to leave this place- the equilibrium must never be broken…'

Yet again, the figure dissolved into thin air and flames flew up between Sir Beagle and the outside world. Sir Beagle's patience was running out by now and he no longer had the strength nor the patience to carry on. What had he done to deserve all this? Why was all of this happening out of the blue? He could not bear the idea of being stuck within the four walls of Dardania so in his last attempt he headed for the South gateway. By now, the deep, dark night reigned over the empty houses of Dardania.

Walking down from the East gateway down to the South one he did not meet a soul and he recalled how none of the gateways were guarded, not a soul in sight. The entire exhibition had disappeared along with the whole population of Dardania. What was going on? Was it really the end of the world? On arrival, he saw how the South gateway was totally empty, abandoned but with all the knick knacks still there on the stalls, all the furniture in the houses, the caravans, everything left exactly as it was, everything except for the human beings. Sir Beagle had only one choice left: to open the last gateway seemed the only way to put an end to this nightmare and uncover the truth. He pushed the gateway door with all his might but another cloud swallowed up the outer world. All of a sudden, the outline of a lizard appeared wrapped in cloud so Sir Beagle was only able to see its shadow and hear its deep voice.

'Man, do not leave the city, don't let fire abandon this place, the equilibrium must never be broken…'

Then something unusual happened. The cloud dissolved and on the other side of it appeared a night sky, trees and green lawns lit by the light of the stars. However, Sir Beagle did not have the time to admire all this as he had already fled into the maze of streets of Dardania, on the verge of desperation in his efforts to find a way out of this place that had always existed but he could no longer find.

Next morning a tepid Autumn sun shone over the spires and towers of Dardania. The usual hustle and bustle had already started on every road with the scent of doing business in the air. However, in a corner where the sun's rays did not reach a dirty narrow alley, Sir Beagle sat squatting all wrapped up in layers of dusty blankets. He was awake with his eyes wide open staring into the void. The words of the four figures echoed and echoed in his head; it was a real nightmare. He had tried to get up during the night but then decided it would be better to stay put until dawn. Hours and hours of reflection had helped him a lot and he had come to the conclusion, by intuition, that everything that had happened the previous night must have had something to do with that cross, that damn cross with no value whatsoever. He might have been wrong, but then he would have given anything, even his gold tooth to get out of this prison. Then without thinking twice, he got up onto his feet, and taking a decisive step even if he was a bit shaky, he walked toward the West gateway. The main road was just as busy and crowded as it had been the day before, so many people, but despite this Sir Beagle didn't take any notice. His tired eyes and dirty sweaty skin gave way his obvious suffering but at the same time he seemed absent, unaware of the world around him. Sir Beagle's only goal was to find the gateway and his freedom. He stopped right in front of it, just where the shark had appeared at the beginning. He stood still looking at the horizon for a few minutes, when a man suddenly patted him on his shoulder. Sir Beagle jumped round, nervous as he was, but keeping his calm. A noble knight in azure armour appeared before him.

'Hello! Is that for sale?'

Sir Beagle did not quite understand what he meant but saw the knight pointing to the cross: he wanted the cross. Sir Beagle could hardly control his joy and handed over the cross as quickly as he could, shouting at the top of his voice.

'Take it! Take it! It is a present. As from today I am a free man!'

And he ran off. The knight, surprised, saw him running away beyond the gateway, through the caravans, out toward the far off horizon, leaping and shouting like a mad man. At last, Sir Beagle would be able to admire once more what he thought he had lost forever, the sea, the land, the sky and the sun.

The purple battle

Battles. The valour of battles. The strength of battles. Bloody battles. The cruelty of battles. Death in battles. How many had there been? A hundred, thousands, millions? One was enough to unleash horror.

The Sacred Army proceeded relentlessly toward the glen. King Harold the Blond had guided his troops audaciously for days on end. Now it was the early hours of the morning and almost time for the decisive clash. The Sun was to guide their swords. The Army of Terror advanced fearlessly, impassive, at a quick pace, behind the slow steps of the General. The black banners swayed in the sad mountain wind, the glen was just down below them. The troops were dressed in armour as black as pitch, skulls dangled over the sides of the horses and the thirst for blood could be clearly seen in their eyes.

The Army of Chaos proceeded in a casual way without any precise order guided by the feared troll Flarg. His soldiers were rough, rather squalid in their red armour. They spat and swore all the time as they devastated everything in their path from vegetation to whole villages. Their roar could be heard from far off; that was their war cry.

The Army of the Secular Oak stood still in the wood, they could not see the glen but it was an excellent hiding place for the time being. The army of tigers was at rest and Prince Greenie was busy studying his next plan of action. He had to put his revenge into action as soon as possible and the surprise element was his best weapon.

The sun was slowly rising in the sky as time passed and the armies moved closer and closer. The Sacred Army appeared on the horizon then stopped waiting for the other armies to appear. The Army of Terror sprung up from behind a hill only a few hundred metres from the glen. The

Army of Chaos, instead, due to its disorganization was split into two groups and came on the scene in two different places. Naturally, the Army of the Secular Oak was not present. Prince Greenie was in the wood and from behind the bushes he had an excellent view of the battlefield.

At midday, the troops of the Sacred Army began marching again after a break for lunch, which lasted two hours. The soldiers' pace was much slower now and they were more nervous. In the distance, they caught glimpse of the black horses of the Army of Terror as they came down the hillside. They looked like a swarm of flies ready to devour their enemies. At the same time, the warriors of evil saw a pure white cloak moving slowly; it was a sight that made their blood boil with anger. In the meantime both from the left side and the right the troops of the Army of Chaos came rumbling down to the foothills like a nuisance: they were ready for a massacre.

The spark that set things off came in the early afternoon for a quite stupid reason. The three armies were now quite close to one another (even the fourth one was close by too although no one knew it). Suddenly one of the Sacred Army soldiers slumped to the ground. His comrades saw him down on one side spitting blood. The reaction was immediate. Everyone turned horrified to the poor soldier who lay dead on the ground. The king noticed the confusion so he came up to the crowd and saw the lifeless body of the soldier.

'Who is to blame?' said the angry king. 'I'm sure it must be one of the soldiers belonging to the Army of Terror who has cast an evil spell over us. We cannot stand for it, my warriors! Let's attack, for the Glory of the Sun!'

The troops' answer was immediate and unanimous: let's attack now!

On the other side of the glen, the Army of Terror had stopped to fight some trolls who had appeared unexpectedly. Nothing to worry about, nothing dangerous but one had to be careful as trolls and goblins were very clever at setting traps and causing panic. Anyway, everything went smoothly and the Army of Terror were able to continue their march of death. Then the Angel of Death blew her horn and everyone's attention, including the General's, turned to watch the Sacred Army galloping toward them. That was their sign; that was the moment. The General announced a mysterious sentence and all the troops answered with a cry: the war had just begun.

The Army of Chaos noticed the lightning movement of the two factions. There was no time to lose and in no time the two troops charged, one toward the Army of Terror, the other toward the Sacred Army. It was time for them to fight.

In contrast, the Army of the Secular Oak still was not ready and it stood there watching the glen, where in a short time hell would break loose.

The impact came in a flash and it was so violent that many died instantly. The armours clashed in a fierce duel body to body together with the clashing sound of their swords. It was sheer confusion at the start, then it turned into a carnage. In just a few minutes, the glen had been turned into a blood bath, full of dead bodies or rather shreds of bodies. The warriors of the Army of Chaos were the most violent, they slaughtered every enemy without pity, some even devoured the bleeding flesh of the bodies spread over the battlefield. The Army of Terror, on the other hand, was sadistic, finding pleasure in causing pain to others. Some soldiers of the Sacred Army were caught with a noose around their necks and dragged on the ground for the whole of the battle. The Army of the Secular Oak watched all this whirl of white, black and red. Time had come for them to put their plan of action into place and in a flash they appeared from behind the bushes running toward the blood bath.

The second impact was just as tremendous. Unfortunately, the plan of the Army of the Secular Oak did not turn out so well. The surprise element worked only partially because the Sacred Army had seen them coming in time; it ended with heavy losses on both sides. No change then: all four armies had undergone heavy losses. Then the situation began to get worse and by sunset no one was left alive, everyone was dead. This may seem strange but there were no survivors. All that remained was a large purple stain in the middle of the glen, the result of an atrocious clash. But was it all worth it? If I were you, I would go and see the soldier of the Sacred Army, the one who died before the battle started. Look carefully at the bloodstain near his mouth and you will see something glimmer: that stupid soldier has swallowed a shard of glass, by mistake, when it fell onto his plate. At times, the price of a battle can be ridiculous.

The strength of the king

Superstition is no joke. At times it can lead you down the road to destruction even if you do not really want to go there. It is difficult to save oneself in time so the best option is probably to forget the whole idea.

Once there was a powerful king who had such strong muscles that he was able to disintegrate a wooden beam in no time at all. He was not evil, but he had the defect of being arrogant due to his notable talents and at times he worried he might lose his strength. One night he had a terrible nightmare, he dreamt about a mysterious figure, a shadow that came to visit him during the night to tell him something important.

You powerful man, king of this people, listen to my message. You are not the strongest of all; there is another man stronger than you. I have seen him with my own eye uproot trees, wipe out whole villages with one breath, turn enormous blocks into dust. Be careful because one day he could come to your castle and destroy everything in sight; your strength will not be enough to stop him.

The king awoke suddenly in a bath of sweat. His worst fear now seemed to be a real threat to his kingdom. The king as a superstitious man when it came to certain things and so he engaged a witch who lived with him in one of the towers of his castle. The witch was a weird sort but everyone admired her for her clever magic. She had solved many of the kingdom's problems, so according to the king she would have no difficulty in solving this problem too. The day after his dream, the king rushed to the witch's door and knocked three times. The old witch opened the door slowly. She was wearing a dark green shawl.

'Oh my Lord, what brings you here?' she said in a weak voice.

'I'm in danger.' replied the king trembling.

He went straight into the room and sat in his usual armchair, the one for guests. The witch was used to the king's mood swings so she made no comment. She simply sat opposite him waiting indifferently. Then the king spoke.

'Witch, my friend, I've discovered that I'm no longer the strongest. There is someone who precedes me, so he is a danger for me and the others!'

'Just a moment, Sir. Before you start to explain, I'd like to remind you that I have not yet been paid as I have should have been...'

'Who cares!' interrupted the King. 'We're talking about my life here!'

'Alright!' replied the old woman sulking.

She got up from his chair and walked toward a table full of flasks, bottles and enormous tomes. She gathered a series of strange objects, closed her eyes and began to meditate. The king waited anxiously. The witch rubbed her hands, said a few magic words then finally opened her eyes. She turned slowly to look at the king.

'The stars say that the strongest man exists and he lives in the mines of Myfors. You are right, Your Majesty, you are in danger!'

'What? Was I right? Well then there is no time to lose!'

He ran down the stairs and quickly gathered his councillors to inform them of the fact. There were various reactions: some protested shouting to the king telling him not to trust the witch, other encouraged him to leave his kingdom immediately for the safety of his people. The king, on seeing how those men who were sceptical about the witch, were precisely those who were hostile toward him, decided to gather up a small army. He took his best knights and some miners with him and set off that very same day.

The mines of Myfors were not far away. They were situated at the feet of the Red Mountains, still a part of the kingdom but they had been uninhabited for years now. They had been called mines ever since the dawn of time, but both the mines and the surrounding areas were now barren and inhospitable. The king had only been there once when he was young but this time he had to return for reasons far more important. He had no idea about how to defeat an invincible person but first he had to identify his number one enemy. After a two-hour hike he came to a fork in the road, one was the main road while the other was nothing more than an unkempt dirt track. The latter was the one that led to the mines, and even though there were no signposts, the king recognised it to be the one. Under a grey and gloomy sky, our heroes set off straight away. The colossal Red Mountains rose steeply in front of them without trees. At the foot of the mountain stood the mine, a disused tunnel almost on the verge of collapse. It did not look very inviting for the miners; a man would need a whole lot of courage to live in a death trap like that. The king however did not listen to their comments; together they entered the dark caverns. The miners of course had brought all the necessary equipment with them, pickaxes, lanterns, ropes and some hope but that mine was not safe at all. Suddenly out of the blue, the cavern walls exploded, it shocked all the squad and many died instantly, and only the king, two knights and one miner survived the explosion. The tunnel filled with smoke which did not give signs of dying down. The four survivors fumbled in the dark, their eyes blinded by the dense smoke. The king tried to flee toward the exit but he hit against a rocky wall and fell to the ground while his distant comrades shouted for help.

Time went by and the king must have remained unconscious for quite a while, dreaming again. The shadow of the night appeared to him again, this time it was wearing a white tunic. To his bitter surprise, the king noticed that under the hood was the face of the witch.

Stupid king! You are the victim of deception, you are finished. You should have satisfied me with the money I asked for, but your pride and arrogance got the better of you. Didn't you see who your real enemy was? Now magic has had its impact and I will be the queen of the new kingdom...

The dream vanished and the king found himself in the dark. He called his comrades by name. No answer. All of a sudden, stones began to fall and the whole mine started to tremble. There was no escape now and fear overcame the boldness of the king, a victim of superstition. He ended up under a heavy pile of debris regretting for evermore the weight of his error.

A trick in the dark

The cemetery was wrapped in fog. Very few people passed by there at that hour, the surroundings were certainly not very cheerful. The house of the living dead in Quinton was famous for being the scene of many brutal murders for satanic motives. Rumours you may say, interesting enough to tickle the curiosity of many, especially those fond of the occult. Richard Thomas was one of these, an apprentice wizard to be precise. After only a few weeks, he had become a member of the Pearly Unicorn Sect. It was not a sect that was appreciated by the inhabitants of Quinton but many of them were a part of it. When the fog came down in the evening, you could hear echoing of their motto far off along the dark streets.

If you believe in the existence of the Unicorn, I will believe in yours.

Also on the evening that Richard Thomas walked to the cemetery gates, the fog hid every single thing. The wind blew softly; it was a freezing cold wind, cold like dead bodies. The branches of the trees swayed slightly in the wind but without any real life, just like dead bodies. The street was empty, no lights only the large lamppost in the small square opposite lit everything. Wherever the light could not reach total darkness reigned ready to rouse who knows what mysterious force from out of nowhere. The cemetery was calm, immersed in silence; the grave headstones lay speechless in the damp grass.

Richard was rather tense but he wanted to show everyone that he was more than just a simple apprentice. Discovering crimes in the cemetery was big stuff and surely would have granted him a satisfactory position. He was now there in front of the rusty gates; it was his moment. But just then a mosquito bit his leg and broke his thoughts. What a nuisance, damn insects! Obviously, he tried not to think about it, he had other things on his mind. So, without stopping a second more in that desolate square, he pulled out a piece of wire from his pocket. Breaking a lock was as easy as pie but it had to be a clean job as what he was about to do was illegal. Neither the lock nor the gate resisted but the deafening grinding of the gate hinges was terrifying. It echoed in the air like a trumpet call and Richard stood still and waited for someone to come out to stop him. No one came. The cemetery went back to sleep in all its deathly silence. Richard could stay calm nobody was around, not even the guardian. The dead had been abandoned by the living and now they were forced to lay in the mud, covered in moss for eternity.

Just inside the cemetery stood two large marble statues, the largest ones in the cemetery. They were not the usual angels, but two rather ambiguous figures: on the right there was a longhaired man wearing a tunic, on the left the usual mysterious figure wearing a cloak and a hood. After about ten steps beyond the statues, he heard a thud. Richard stood still in his steps for a second then slowly turned. He wondered who was out there. A cat, a silly black cat had jumped off the pedestal of the statue of the hooded man. Richard took a sigh of relief. He was about to chuckle to himself when that moment of hilarity turned into terror. Six claws appeared from under the sleeves of the cloak, three on each side. This certainly was no cat, but what was it? His questions were to no avail. All at once, the statue came alive and raised its arms up to the sky. Richard stood there in silence trying to take steps backward but unfortunately he made the mistake of treading on a branch. Hearing the crunch, the statue turned round in a flash. Richard was petrified: he caught glimpse of such a horrible face in the light of the moon. He was not able to run nor scream. He had seen Death in the face. The statue got down from the pedestal and moved toward Richard. He did not say a word. Richard fully realised he was dealing with something paranormal and he needed all the courage he could get. A meeting with Death. Great!

'Erm… Death, I presume.' Richard stuttered.

'You presume right, man of flesh,' replied Death in an underworld tone enough to make one's blood curdle. 'but my real name is Dauthi.'

'Why…erm…hmm…did you call me "man of flesh", if I may…ask?'

'Well, it's logical, isn't it? I don't see many living people in my job. And what are you doing here, in the house of the living dead at this hour?'

Quinton town clock struck twelve times for what seemed like an eternity. It was midnight.

'Erm…I think…I…How shall I put it...I think the living dead really do exist!' said Richard taking the risk.

Death raised his eyebrows, his face remained in the semi darkness but his green eyes sparkled. Silence fell all around and that moment seemed like an eternity. Richard thought he had hit bull's eye the way Death stood there, thinking. Then in the end Death looked at him in the face and his eyes penetrated deep into Richard's. Drops of sweat were trickling down Richard's back and the wind struck up in a grotesque manner for a few seconds, then stopped and silence returned. Death spoke.

'Shame, it means you don't believe in yourself!'

The phrase wheezed like a dagger and Richard died suddenly with a pang in his heart. A moment was enough, time enough to hear the owl howl his funeral lament at a distance as Richard's body fell in the mud and moss. Death remained ice cold, cautiously moved toward the body and pulled out his dagger. He turned to the statue on the right.

'Hey Alfred, it's done. He died instantly. Come out now!'

The statue moved slowly, looked around and got down calmly off the pedestal.

'At last! I was dying of cold. Come on, let's go! Our work here is done.'

' "Another victim in Quinton cemetery" is what we will read in tomorrow's newspaper. "Another soul in honour of the Pearly Unicorn Sect".'

'Oh, stop it' said the other one jokingly and taking off his monstrous mask. This poor idiot was such an easy target.'

'Ok, ok, but let's get out of here now. This place gives me the creeps. Ah, one more thing! Remember we must bring the two real statues back before tomorrow morning.'

The two turned for the last time to look at Richard's body lying there.

'There, you see.' said Dauthi. ' "Killed by the hand of destiny", "Suspended between Life and Death: another curtain closes on the brutal crime scenes for satanic motives". This would sound good in tomorrow's papers.'

The moon shone in the sky for the last time and then disappeared behind the clouds. The wind stopped in deathly silence and the fog thickened once more- Quinton disappeared into thin air…it was another trick in the dark.

A simple question

The two dwarf warriors sat at a table at the bottom of the room. That was their usual place and nobody in the Inn of the Drunk Keeper ever questioned whatever they decided. They were called Peter and Venters, but hardly anyone knew who was Peter and who was Venters. They were not particularly talkative types, just the odd word spoken at the bar, nothing more. They were solitary souls who wandered around the streets every single day always together. Some said they were soldier veterans from the wars in the North but no one could confirm it. The two were inseparable and they hated the presence of strangers. It was for this reason that in the evenings they hid themselves away in the darkest corner of the inn sipping beer, chatting in low voices.

I did not know these two and it was the first time I had set foot in that village, known to be the worst in the area. As I went inside the two were sitting at the end of the room as usual. However, before going up to them, I drank two full glasses of whisky, just the right thing to do considering the upcoming operation. I stood still for a few seconds and then I took those decisive steps towards their table. The noise in the inn died down as silence took over. Everyone was surely watching me as I bravely reached the darkest part of the room. Even the dwarfs noticed me and their look did not do anything to reassure me. It took a lot of courage to sit opposite them and say a simple 'Hello!'. Their reaction was absolute indifference, except for a threatening look. I knew I was not welcome but I had to meet them, it was the only way for me to understand. I coughed a couple of times but there was no reaction. The third time however, I got an immediate reply. One of the dwarfs jumped up and stared, pointing his dagger at me. The situation was getting critical. I tried my best not to lose my calm; as long as I could say the right thing at the right moment, I would have avoided being stabbed in that terrible hole of a place. Stunned, my mind just seemed to be blank. The only way out was rather risky but surely it could not get any worse than this so I whispered my bold phrase.

'War veterans shouldn't be treated this way!'

The expression on one of the dwarves' face changed at once. He hid the dagger under the table and sat down again. There was a moment's silence then the buzz in the inn started up again among the astonished looks and comments of the onlookers. Someone had finally managed to sit with the two dwarfs. Peter and Venters had been so struck by my sentence that it had made them change their attitude toward me. The one who had got up first was now sitting and thinking. He was the one who broke the silence.

'You've found us. It's been a long time. I thought we were long forgotten by the Ministry of War.'

I still hadn't really caught on to what they were talking about so I had to be careful with my answers.

'I know, I know. We've only just found you. As you can see I'm not here in an official capacity, I didn't want everyone to know.'

'Yes, but you've certainly made yourself known now, haven't you?' answered the dwarf. 'We have no friends here in the village. We try to keep away from this group of ignorant country folk.'

'I see.' I continued keeping a serious tone. 'But the only thing I don't understand is: what have you been doing all this time since the end of the war till now?'

I wanted to keep war out of the discussion because it was not exactly clear to me which war it was.

'Wouldn't it be more fair to ask what happened during the war?'

The story was starting to get interesting. I did not say anything. What was important now was for me to keep my ears well and truly open.

'Well,' began the dwarf. 'after the Battle of Dameon in the lands of the North the whole army split up. Our troop sheltered in the Forest of Thunder. There were no great losses of life fortunately but we suffered the cold and exhaustion. Venters and myself had the duty to explore the surrounding area and worn out every single enemy. During the exploration, the raiders of Erg managed to take our comrades by surprise and exterminate them all. Of course, a few of the raiders noticed our absence and came looking for us, chasing us. In the meantime, unaware of everything, we kept running. It was only when we could hear the raiders shouting that we realized they were not far behind us and we were in danger. We ran as fast as we could but the forest was immense and it would have taken days to find a way out. Not knowing where to go, we hid in the first place we came across. Just a few meters from us we could hear the gushing water of what sounded like a waterfall, but it turned out to be nothing more than a simple stream that ended up in a small lake below. We decided to jump; it was our only way to safety. The raiders soon realized our plan. Jumping was not enough; we had to find a place to hide. That was when Venters lost his balance and fell into the water and down the waterfall, hitting his head against the rocky wall.'

At that point, Venters broke in with a laugh and he continued the rest of the story.

'Pete didn't see me come back up to the surface, so he dived in to save me. Behind the veil of water, there was a magnificent natural grotto. It was so beautiful. I ended up at the entrance to the cave. Thank God, I hadn't broken any bones! I turned round and saw Pete beyond the waterfall. I whistled to him to come over and he understood straight away that I had found a suitable hiding place. It was no ordinary hiding place, as we soon found out. We had ended up in the dwelling of a hermit. I still remember him to this day, sitting there at the end of the cave, muttering senseless phrases. He was scared at first but he soon realized our good intentions and welcomed us with open arms. We called him a hermit but he was simply an explorer. He had hidden there for a reason. After a recent journey in eastern lands, he had finally discovered the Djinn, the Sense of Life and all things belonging to the Universe. Unfortunately, the answer to his question had traumatized him to the point that he felt he had to hide from the world. At first, we thought he was joking but then he wanted to explain everything and now nothing is the same. In a flash, a sentence brought the world crashing down. If I could go back in time, I wouldn't do what I did again.'

The story ended here. I was struck by it. Some things were not clear but the psychological condition of the dwarfs was quite disturbed. I had a load of questions I would have liked to ask them, but it was getting late so there was only time for one more. Goodness knows why I chose that question but it came naturally when I asked him.

'What is the Djinn?'

One of the dwarfs got up slowly, placed his lips near my ear and whispered a word. It was a moment. That said, I was even more struck, upset I would say. Everything I had believed in suddenly came crashing down. I felt I had to escape, but where to? There wasn't anywhere to go. But I wanted to flee; I couldn't stand it there any longer. I stood up and said goodbye to both Pete and Venters.

'Goodbye! I'll let you know about the Ministry of War as soon as possible.'

'Let us know.' said Pete. 'We already know everything and that's why we've sacrificed our lives, just like valorous soldiers. It's a high price to pay!'

I left the inn in a hurry, glad to leave it all behind me. Who had the courage to look people in the face? Let alone talk to them? Nothing had any sense any more. Maybe I should have let things drop from the very start but man is a curious being to the point of annihilating himself in a fraction of a second.

The Inn of the Drunken Keeper still exists if you are interested and the two dwarves have never moved from there. Would you like to know what the Djinn is, by any chance?

The crossroads

The souls felt alone as soon as the usual morning mist floated down over the paths in the wood. Their bodies were decomposing now under the moist soil; they had been wandering aimlessly for some time looking for help. They walked in single file without making the slightest sound. They all looked the same from afar but close up it was possible to recognize doctors, lawyers, tradesmen and commanders or even simple folk. Some thought they were still alive and continued talking about their future projects; then there were those who wanted to go back home, even though they no longer had one.

They had only a short wait. From a distance it was possible to vaguely make out the flames coming from two torches. The Guardians of the Faith had finally arrived and Destiny was with them. All the guardians were hooded, wearing white tunics and had a gold rope around their necks. Two of them walked at the front of the cortege holding the funeral torches up high, behind them there were another two carrying a stretcher bearing the bronze mask of Destiny. The last guardian ended the cortege; he was carrying a tangled mass of trinkets and baubles which made clanging sounds to the rhythm of the wind. It all created a mystic atmosphere. The souls were still not ready for this moment and some even feared the forthcoming verdict. This verdict was based on the Equality of Mangara, a sort of eye for an eye principle but very different from the Muslim tradition. It involved weighing up guilt and goodness so as to make them all equal. It was then Destiny's turn to make the fair decision.

The bronze mask was now in front of the souls, disquieting as ever, ready to do justice. The guardians broke out into a Gregorian chant then silence returned. Only a few seconds passed. Suddenly, out of the group of frightened souls came a bald headed man. The two guardians holding the torches made a sign to keep back but he stopped directly facing them.

'Destiny, fate that guides men, I am Jeff A. Menges, Secretary of State of the Republic of Rodomontea. I come in sign of peace to negotiate with you, oh Divine!'

The souls were astonished. To face up to Destiny in this way took a great deal of courage. Souls muttering in the background could be heard, but it soon stopped when a deep voice pealed out threateningly.

Mortal, your audacity toward me is unprecedented! However, according to the Principles of the Equity of Mangara. I shall listen to your plea.

Fortunately, Menges's risky action did not cause any ugly surprises, or at least not then. The officer, glad to have been given permission to speak, took a deep breath and said his fatal words.

'I, Jeff A. Menges, wish to return to the land of the living in order to comply with the Equity of Mangara. I wish to have complete authoritarian control of my people and at the same time make them happy with my virtue. In this city of perfect government, I shall be their freedom. This is my desire, oh Divine.'

There was a slight pause, a long pause. The scene stood still, tense at this crucial point. The bronze mask was only an object but a certain expression could be envisaged in those metal eyes, something apocalyptic.

You, Mortal, you are only a man full of his own importance. You consider yourself a giant, capable of governing the world but you are not able to even see what is under your shoes where people leave their happiness and die in a sad world. People have to know their own virtue, not yours.

Just then, thunder roared in the sky. A demon sprung out from nowhere, caught hold of the poor officer and took him away deep into the dark forest. Final justice came quickly for poor Menges. There was no longer any mist only a fine drizzle slightly stinging. The panic had vanished now but the souls were still horrified. The guardians and Destiny instead stood still like statues. The ritual continued in a normal fashion; no one asked any more questions and some endured their punishments in silence while others enjoyed their rewards. Nobody wanted to know where Menges had ended up. Only after the celebrations, Destiny announced his last words of the day.

That man before, is now history. He was so busy trying to find a better life that he has lost his body and soul. Now, he is in the city of illusions, in the city of disappointment trying to find his lost smile in the utopian world of the living.

The bronze mask shone brilliantly in the sun shining in the sky. The bad weather had cleared and the sun shone brilliantly in a clear blue sky. The souls, covered in a golden veil, followed the cortege of the Guardians of the Faith with a smile on their lips, finally free of their worries, ready to take that new journey into Eternal Sleep.

Spring 2000

www.ingramcontent.com/pod-product-compliance
Lightning Source LLC
Chambersburg PA
CBHW071517030726
47593CB00003B/1300